SILLYVILLE OR BUST

by Peter Hannan

Alfred A. Knopf, Publisher New York

THIS IS A BORZOI BOOK PUBLISHED BY ALFRED A. KNOPF, INC.

Library of Congress Cataloging-in-Publication Data
Hannan, Peter.
  Sillyville or bust / by Peter Hannan.
    p.   cm.
  Summary: Ruby and her brother's boring car trip with Aunt Ida and
Uncle Gus turns exciting when they make an unscheduled stop in
Sillyville.
  ISBN 0-679-80285-1 (pbk.)—ISBN 0-679-90285-6 (lib. bdg.)
  [1. Travel—Fiction.   2. Humorous stories.]   I. Title.
PZ7.H1978Si   1991
[E]—dc20   89-35342   CIP   AC

Manufactured in the United States of America
10   9   8   7   6   5   4   3   2   1

This book is dedicated to my father, who once sailed a boat through a grocery-store window, and to my mother, who once said, "How could the engine be missing? The car wouldn't even *run* if the engine were missing!"

O ne summer, my sister Ruby and I were asked
to endure a very long car ride home with
Aunt Ida and Uncle Gus.

We were miserable. To call these people dull
would be an insult to dull people.

As we pulled out of the driveway Aunt Ida remarked, "Remember now, youngsters, your uncle needs to concentrate, so no monkeyshines."

For the first three hours we rode without speaking a word. Ruby was lucky enough to finally fall asleep.

I suffered in silence.

BLAH
BLAH
BLAH
BLAH
BLAH

Aunt Ida said, "So, little man, what are your thoughts, careerwise? You won't be in the fourth grade forever, you know."

I pretended to be dozing.

An hour later I tried to tell a joke, but Aunt Ida interrupted. "We don't like jokes or riddles. We don't get them."

I prayed we'd have a flat tire—just for a break in the monotony.

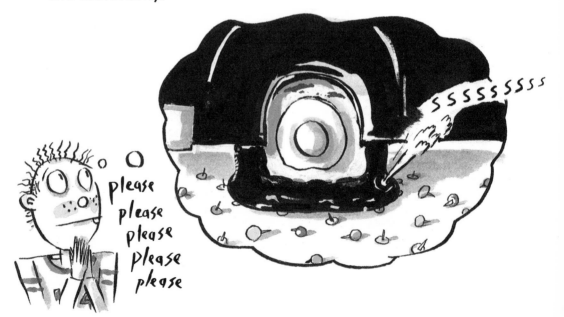

SSSSSSSSS

please
please
please
please
please

Ruby woke up and asked if we could stop to eat.

"We'll make a seven-minute stop in Drabville for rest rooms and gas only," said Uncle Gus.

"We have my own delicious sandwiches for lunch," said Aunt Ida.

The sandwiches tasted like wet dirt. We tried to choke them down, but they made us gag.

The view out the window was no help.

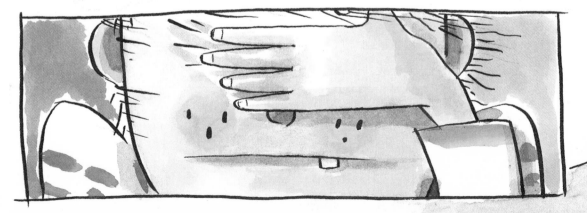

But one billboard caught my eye.

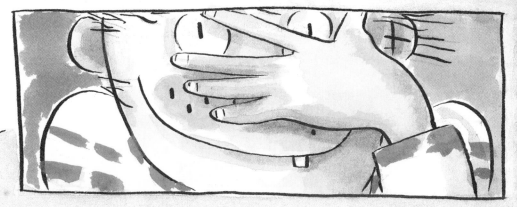

"Ida, how far to Drabville?" asked Uncle Gus. Aunt Ida opened the map and kind of lost control of it. It blew right into my uncle's face.

"Ida, take the wheel!" cried Uncle Gus.
Aunt Ida grabbed the wheel and shouted,
"I can't see either!"

Uncle Gus and Aunt Ida finally got themselves untangled...just as we crashed through a grocery store window.

Uncle Gus was completely covered with mashed fruit.

"Yuck, that's gross," said Ruby.

"And I'm a little grocer!" said a man with an odd mustache. Ruby and I fell down laughing.

"We don't get it," said Aunt Ida and Uncle Gus.

"Welcome. I'm the mayor of Sillyville," someone
else said.

"Why are you dressed like a mouse?" asked
Uncle Gus.

"Gerbil," the mayor replied.

"Mouse, gerbil, whatever—it's still *silly*," said
Aunt Ida.

"Thank you very much!" said the mayor.

"We'll have your car fixed in a jiffy," said a
mechanic in a wedding gown.

"I'd like an estimate first," said Uncle Gus.

"No charge," said the mechanic.

"Don't be silly!" said Aunt Ida.

"I have to be!" said the mechanic as she drove
the car back through the window and down the
street.

VRROOOOM!

A policeman with a rubber nose hopped in on one foot and sang, "You're all under arrest."

"For what?" we cried.

"Making applesauce without a license," he whispered. He carted us off to the Sillyville jail.

In jail, Aunt Ida and Uncle Gus seemed a little low. We were visited by the jail doctor, who prescribed a macaroni bath for all of us.

They woke us up early in the morning to go to court. After reviewing the evidence, the judge said we would have to spend the rest of our lives in the Sillyville jail. That is, unless each of us did something immediately that was really silly....

"But we've never done anything silly in our lives," said Aunt Ida, trembling.

"I'll go first," said Ruby.

The jury was ready!!!

Then she hung upside down from the ceiling fan
and whistled a Beatles medley.

I did my famous lunatic rabbit imitation.

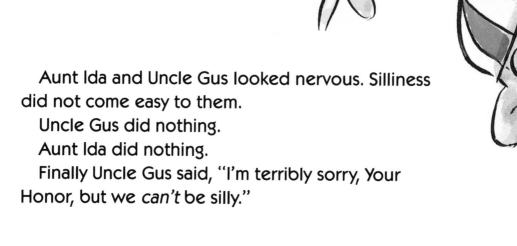

Aunt Ida and Uncle Gus looked nervous. Silliness did not come easy to them.

Uncle Gus did nothing.

Aunt Ida did nothing.

Finally Uncle Gus said, "I'm terribly sorry, Your Honor, but we *can't* be silly."

"We've always thought of it as being rather foolish and unproductive," added Aunt Ida.

"That's the silliest statement I've ever heard," said the judge. He hit himself on the head and shouted, "Case dismissed!"

Uncle Gus and Aunt Ida smiled. I think.
We ran out of the courthouse and found the
car waiting.

Ruby and I slept the rest of the way home. And when Aunt Ida and Uncle Gus dropped us off, I was sure I had dreamed the whole thing.